Mrs. Patty Is Batty!

Dan Gutman

Pictures by
Jim Paillot

HarperTrophy®
An Imprint of HarperCollins Publishers

Mrs. Patty Is Batty!

Text copyright © 2006 by Dan Gutman

Illustrations copyright © 2006 by Jim Paillot

Library of Congress Cataloging-in-Publication Data is available.

ISBN-10: 0-06-085380-8 (pbk.) — ISBN-13: 978-0-06-085380-8 (pbk.)

ISBN-10: 0-06-085381-6 (lib. bdg.) — ISBN-13: 978-0-06-085381-5 (lib. bdg.)

❖

First Harper Trophy edition, 2006

Visit us on the World Wide Web!

www.harpercollinschildrens.com

17 18 19 20 OPM 40 39 38 37 36 35 34 33 32 31

To Emma

Contents

Mischief Night

My name is A.J. and I hate school.

Well, I have to tell the truth. There is *one* thing about school that I really *love*.

Dismissal! That's when we get to go home!

"Don't forget to wear your Halloween costumes tomorrow," Mrs. Patty cackled over the loudspeaker just before the three o'clock bell rang. "Halloween is my favorite holiday!"

She's not kidding. Mrs. Patty celebrates Halloween all year long. There are always cobwebs and spiders covering her desk. She wears earrings that look like little skeletons. And she always has candy in her office. Lots of candy.

I like Mrs. Patty. She's the secretary at Ella Mentry School. That means she sits in the front office all day and makes announcements over the loudspeaker. "Friday is pizza day!" she will say. Or "Miss Lazar, please mop up the throw up in the vomitorium." Or "Will the children who left their jackets in the playground please remove their clothes."

Being a school secretary is like being a DJ. That is a cool job.

I grabbed a piece of candy and ran out the front door of Ella Mentry School with my friends Ryan and Michael. Free at last!

"What should we do for mischief night tonight?" asked Ryan, who once ate a piece of the seat cushion on the school bus.

"Let's T.P. somebody's house," said Michael, who never ties his shoes.

"Yeah!"

I don't know if you know this or not, but the night before Halloween is mischief night. That's the night you go out and do mischief, so it has the perfect name. And T.P. stands for toilet paper. On mischief night you go out and throw toilet paper all over people's trees. That's the first rule of being a kid.

"Whose house should we T.P.?" I asked.

"How about Miss Daisy's house?" Ryan suggested. (Miss Daisy is our teacher.)

"Nah," Michael said, "we'd get in big trouble."

"How about Mr. Klutz's house?" Ryan suggested. (Mr. Klutz is our principal.)

"Nah," Michael said, "we'd get in even *bigger* trouble."

Speaking of trouble, guess who ran by

us at that very moment? It was the most annoying person in the history of the world, little Miss Perfect Andrea Young. She is in our class and has curly brown hair. She thinks she is so smart.

"What's the rush, Andrea?" asked Ryan.

"I have to finish my homework before ballet class," Andrea said.

"Why don't you do your homework *after* ballet class?" Michael asked.

"After ballet class I have soccer and my cooking class."

Andrea takes classes in everything. If they gave a class in going to the bathroom, she would take that class so she could get better at it. I hate her.

But seeing Andrea gave me the greatest idea in the history of the world.

"Let's T.P. Andrea's house!" I told the guys.

"A.J., you're a genius!" said Ryan.

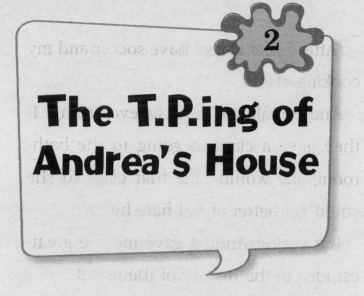

The T.P.ing of Andrea's House

After dinner I told my parents I was going down the street to Ryan's house. Ryan told his parents he was going down the street to my house. But me and Ryan didn't go over to each other's houses at all. We both went to Andrea's house. Our parents didn't have to know we were going out for mischief night. But Michael couldn't come. He was grounded for pulling the arms off his sister's doll.

Me and Ryan each brought a roll of toilet paper in our backpacks.

"This is gonna be great!" Ryan whispered as we hid behind a car across the street from Andrea's house. "Andrea's gonna wake up in the morning and find the trees in her yard are covered in toilet paper!"

I couldn't stop giggling.

"It will be the greatest day in the history of the world," I said.

It was starting to get dark out, but we still had to be careful because we didn't want to get caught. My friend Billy who lives around the corner told me that if you get caught T.P.ing somebody's house, the police put you in a jail with *no* toilet paper. Yuck! But Billy is a big liar anyway.

Me and Ryan tiptoed to Andrea's front lawn like we were spies on a mission. It was cool.

"Be careful not to spit on the ground," I whispered as we pulled the rolls of toilet paper out of our backpacks.

"Why not?" Ryan asked.

"You don't want to leave any DNA evidence," I said. "They could scoop up our spit and prove it came from us."

"Good thinking," he agreed.

I'm in the gifted and talented program at school, so I'm constantly thinking up genius stuff like that. Andrea is in the gifted and talented program too (of course).

There's a really big tree in Andrea's front yard. It has a lot of branches, so it's perfect for hanging toilet paper. We decided to loop the toilet paper over the high branches first. After that we would drape it over the low branches until the whole tree was covered.

"Okay," I said, once we were in position. "Ready . . . aim . . . *fire*!"

I threw my roll of toilet paper as high as I could. Ryan threw his roll of toilet paper at the same time. Both rolls went sailing up into the tree. But there was just one problem. Those toilet paper rolls didn't unroll!

One of the toilet paper rolls bounced off Andrea's house. The other one got stuck in the tree somewhere. It never came down. Bummer in the summer!

"What did we do wrong?" Ryan asked.

"I guess we should have unrolled them a little before we threw them," I said.

"*Now* you tell me!" said Ryan.

We were going to pick up the toilet paper roll and try again. But suddenly a

light went on inside Andrea's house. Andrea stuck her head out the window. Me and Ryan ran and hid behind the tree.

"Shhhh!" Ryan whispered. "I don't think she saw us."

"Daddy!" I heard Andrea yell. "Somebody is outside throwing stuff at our house!"

"Run for it!" I told Ryan. We didn't stop running until we got home.

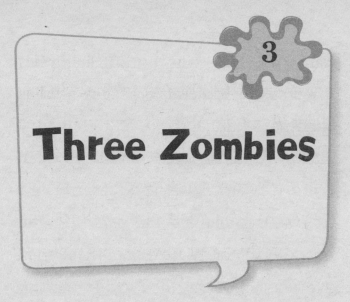

Three Zombies

The next day was October 31, my favorite day of the year. Do you know why October 31 is my favorite day of the year?

I'm not going to tell you.

Okay, okay, I'll tell you.

Because it's Halloween, and that's my favorite holiday. Well, I guess my *favorite* holidays are my birthday and Christmas, because I get presents. But on Halloween you get candy, which is almost as good as getting presents.

Halloween is so great. Think about it. All you have to do is walk around in a silly costume and people give you free candy.* What could be better than that? It's a whole holiday devoted to getting candy! Whoever thought up Halloween was a genius. If you ask me, that guy should get the No Bell Prize. (That's a prize they give out to celebrate the invention of the first bell.)

*Hey, all year long they tell us *not* to take candy from strangers, and then Halloween comes and you *have* to. What's up with that?

When I marched up the front steps to school, Mrs. Patty was standing in the hallway. She was dressed up like a witch. She had a long bent nose with a huge wart on it. How did that wart stay on? She must have glued it or something. It was gross.

"I'll get you, my pretty," she shrieked, waving her broomstick at this girl named Annette, "and your little dog, too!"

"I don't even have a dog," Annette told her.

The front steps were filled with kids dressed as SpongeBobs and Batmans and Oompa-Loompas and all kinds of other weird creatures. Michael was wearing his peewee football uniform, and he had an ax sticking out of his helmet with fake blood running down the side. It was cool.

"What are you supposed to be?" Mrs. Patty asked him.

"I'm a football player," Michael said.

"Why do you have an ax sticking out of your helmet?"

"I'm a *zombie* football player."

"Ooh, that's scary!" said Mrs. Patty.

Ryan was wearing his hockey uniform, and he had an ax sticking out of his helmet with fake blood running down the side.

"Don't tell me," Mrs. Patty said to him.

"You're a zombie hockey player, right?"

"How did you know?" asked Ryan.

"Lucky guess," she said. "What are you supposed to be, A.J.?"

I was dressed up like a penguin who was wearing a space helmet that had an ax sticking out of it and fake blood running down the side. Penguins are cool.

"I'm a killer zombie penguin from outer space," I told her.

"Ooh, that's *very* scary!" said Mrs. Patty. "Be sure to come trick-or-treating at my house after school. I'm going to have more candy than anyone in town. My address is 176 Norman Road."

"We'll be there!" I said.

We were putting our backpacks into our cubbies when little Miss I Know Everything and her equally annoying crybaby friend, Emily, came in. Andrea was dressed up like a ballerina, so of course Miss Show-off had to spin around on her toes to let everybody know she could dance. What is her problem?

Emily was dressed up like a queen. She had a crown on her head, and this long robe that trailed behind her on the floor. What's up with that?

"It's called a train," Emily told us.

"No it's not," I said. "A train is something you ride in that goes *choo-choo*."

Everyone laughed even though I didn't say anything funny.

I thought those girls' costumes were lame. They weren't scary at all. It would have been a lot cooler if they had axes sticking out of their heads like us.

"What are you boys supposed to be?" Emily asked me and Ryan and Michael.

"None of your beeswax," I told her.

"We're zombies," Ryan said.

"I don't think children should be allowed to wear violent costumes on Halloween," Andrea said.

"Can you possibly be any more boring?" I asked her.

"You're dumbheads," said Andrea.

"We are not!"

"Are too!"

We went back and forth like that for a

while until I had to say, "So is your face" to Andrea. Any time anyone says something mean to you, just say "So is your face" to shut them up. That's the first rule of being a kid.

"Hey, Arlo," said Andrea. "I brought a present for you." (She calls me by my real name because she knows how much I hate it.)

Ryan and Michael started giggling.

"Oooooh!" Ryan said. "Andrea brought A.J. a present! They must be in *love!*"

"When are you gonna get married?" asked Michael.

If those guys weren't my best friends, I would hate them.

Andrea opened her backpack and took out a roll of toilet paper.

"You must have dropped this outside my house last night," Andrea said. "I guess you were having a bathroom emergency."

I hate her. Why can't a truck full of toilet paper fall on her head?

Andrea handed me the roll. I didn't know what to say. I didn't know what to do. I had to think fast.

"I wasn't at your house last night," I lied. "I was at my class class."

"Class class?" she asked. "What's that?"

"It's a class that makes you better at taking classes," I told her. "You should take it."

"There's no such thing as a class class," said Emily.

"Hey Emily," I said, pointing under her desk, "look under there!"

"Under where?" asked Emily.

"Ha-ha-ha!" I yelled. "Emily said 'underwear'!"

Everybody cracked up because I made Emily say "underwear." It was hilarious. Any time you can get somebody to say "underwear," you should get the No Bell Prize.

"You're mean!" Emily said. Then she started crying and went running out of the room.

Emily is weird.

Finally our teacher Miss Daisy came in. "Enough chitchat," she said. Miss Daisy was dressed up as a giant brown ball. Only her head, arms, and legs were sticking out.

"What are you supposed to be, Miss Daisy?" everybody asked.

"Guess."

"A basketball?" guessed Ryan.

"Nope."

"A giant poop?" guessed Neil, who we call the nude kid even though he wears clothes.

"Nope," Miss Daisy said. "I'm a big bonbon!" (Bonbons are these chocolate treats Miss Daisy loves.)

"That's a great costume, Miss Daisy," said Andrea, who never misses the chance to brownnose a grown-up.

"Oh, this is no costume," Miss Daisy said. "I ate so many bonbons that I turned into one."

I'm pretty sure she was kidding.

The Emperor Has No Clothes

It's really hard to concentrate on school-work when your teacher is dressed up like a giant bonbon. All I could think about was the candy I would be getting when we went trick-or-treating after school. My mouth was watering. But Miss Daisy was trying her best to teach us.

"If you go trick-or-treating and they give out Kit Kats at five houses and Milky Ways at three houses and Hershey bars at seven houses, how many candy bars will you have altogether? A.J.?"

"Is anybody giving out Snickers?" I asked.

"That's irrelevant," said Miss Daisy.

"No it's not," I told her. "An elephant is a big animal with a long trunk."

Everybody laughed even though I didn't say anything funny.

"I hate Snickers," said Neil the nude kid. "My favorite candy bar is Three Musketeers."

"Let's try to stay on task, shall we?" said

Miss Daisy. Teachers are always telling us to stay "on task." That means we have to talk about boring stuff instead of interesting stuff, like candy bars.

"I like Twizzlers," said Ryan.

"Twizzlers aren't candy bars," Michael said. "They're licorice."

"Ugh! Licorice is yucky," said Neil the nude kid. "It gives candy a bad name."

We went on like that for a while. Nobody could agree on which candy bar was the best. After a while Miss Daisy gave up trying to teach anything.

"All this math talk is making me hungry," she said.

We were all excited to march around

in our costumes, but Miss Daisy said it wasn't time yet.

Finally, after a million hundred years, an announcement came over the loud-speaker.

"It's time for the parade!" Mrs. Patty exclaimed. "Please bring all classes to the playground."

"Yay!" everybody yelled.

Miss Daisy told us to line up boy-girl-boy-girl-boy-girl. (I think she does that so each of us has to be next to somebody we hate.) I had to stand behind annoying Emily, the queen of crybabies. We marched in single file to the playground. The whole school was out there in their costumes.

It was cool. Even the grown-ups were dressed up. Ms. Hannah, our art teacher, dressed up like a famous artist named Picasso. Miss Small, our gym teacher, dressed up like a famous baseball player named Babe Ruth. Mrs. Kormel, our bus driver, dressed up like a famous NASCAR racer named Jeff Gordon. Mrs. Roopy, our librarian, dressed up like a famous children's book author who I never heard of before. Authors are boring.

A lot of the parents came out to see the parade. I saw my mom near the monkey bars. She waved and took a picture of me in my penguin costume.

We marched all the way around the playground. I thought that would be the

end of the parade, but then we had to march around the playground *again*. It was starting to get boring. I was sweating in my penguin costume. I was tired. I didn't want to march anymore. My space helmet was fogged up, and it was getting hard to see out of it. I was sick of the dumb parade. I just wanted to go trick-or-treating and get candy. I *needed* candy!

But that's when the most amazing thing in the history of the world happened. I stepped on Emily's queen costume.

I didn't *mean* to step on Emily's queen costume. Really! I was minding my own business, marching around the play-ground. But her dumb train thing was dragging on the ground behind her and I couldn't see through my space helmet and I guess I got too close to her and I stepped on the train.

It would have been okay, except that Emily kept right on walking, like she didn't even know I was standing on her train. What a dumbhead! Anyway, it must have been some cheap costume, because it ripped really easily. The next thing anybody knew, Emily's whole costume was on the ground and not on Emily.

"Look!" somebody shouted. "Underwear!"

Well, the only thing funnier than getting someone to *say* "underwear" is actually *seeing* someone in their underwear.

That's the first rule of being a kid. And Emily was standing in the middle of the playground in her underwear! There were even flowers on it!

Everybody was pointing and laughing. It was hilarious! A real Kodak moment. And we saw it live and in person. You

should have been there. I hope my mom took a picture.

"Eeeeeeeeeeeeeek!" Emily screamed. "A.J. stepped on my train!"

"It's a train wreck," I said. "Get it?"

But Emily didn't think my joke was very funny. She started crying (of course) and went running off the playground. I don't even know where she went.

Well, nah-nah-nah boo-boo on Emily. That's what she gets for dressing up like a dumb queen anyway.

"I Rule the School!"

We marched around the playground for about a million hundred hours. Finally the dumb parade was over and we could go home.

Or at least I *thought* we could go home. First we all had to go back inside the school and sit in the all-purpose room.

There was a fancy chair up on the stage. It was like one of those chairs you see in a palace.

When all the classes were seated, music started playing and some tall guy came into the all-purpose room dressed up like a king. He was wearing a gold cape, and he was holding a big sword.

It was Mr. Klutz, our principal! Even though he was wearing a crown on his head, I knew it was him because he is completely bald. I mean *completely*.

"Off with their heads!" Mr. Klutz shouted as he marched down the center aisle. "Let them eat cake!"

Miss Daisy told us that, in the old days,

kings were constantly chopping off people's heads and making them eat cake. That must have been a cool time to live. I like to eat cake, but I don't think I would like the chopping-off-your-head part very much.

"I rule the school," Mr. Klutz announced as he sat in the fancy chair. "Quiet down or you will be thrown in the dungeon in the basement."

That was a complete lie. Everybody knows the dungeon is on the third floor.

"Cool costume, Mr. Klutz!" some kid yelled.

"Silence!" Mr. Klutz hollered. "I know not this Klutz person of whom you speak. I am King Louis the Fourteenth of France."

"Why are you dressed up like a king?" Ryan asked.

"As king," he replied, "I need not

worry about parent-teacher conferences and behavior problems and head lice and bus schedules and test scores. I am all powerful. What I say goes."

Mr. Klutz was talking just like a real king. It was cool.

After he finished acting all kinglike, he talked to us about Halloween safety. He told us to have fun trick-or-treating, but to look both ways before we crossed the street. He said we shouldn't go inside any strange houses, and we shouldn't eat any candy that isn't wrapped up.

"What should we do if we come to a house and they don't give us any candy?"

asked one of the third graders.

"Off with their heads!" said Mr. Klutz.

"What if some kids don't get any candy?" asked one of the first graders.

"Let them eat cake!"

Mr. Klutz enjoyed being king a little too much, if you ask me.

I couldn't wait to get out of school because, well, I can't wait to get out of school *every* day. But this day was special because we would be going trick-or-treating and getting candy.

Finally the bell rang and we got out of jail . . . I mean, school. Everybody poured out the front door.

"Free at last!" Michael shouted.

"It's candy time!" Ryan yelled.

Mrs. Patty was standing on the front steps of the school in her witch costume. Her wart still didn't fall off. She told us again that we should make sure to trick-or-treat at her house because she has more candy than anyone in town.

"And remember," she said, "don't let the Halloween Monster catch you."

The *what?*

44

"I've never heard of the Halloween Monster," I said.

"Oh sure," said Mrs. Patty. "Every year the Halloween Monster chops up kids, steals their candy, and keeps it for himself."

Yikes! The Halloween Monster? I looked at Michael. Michael looked at Ryan. Ryan looked at me. Then we all tore out of there as fast as we could.

Giant Bananas and Two-headed Astronauts

This was the first Halloween that me and Michael and Ryan were allowed to go trick-or-treating without our parents. We went home to drop off our backpacks and get pillowcases to hold all the candy. Then we met up again at Michael's house.

"Let's go!" Ryan said. "If I don't eat a

Twizzler in about five minutes, I'm gonna die."

"Not so fast," Michael said, opening up a big map he had drawn. "I worked it all out so we'll have the maximum candy accumulation."

Wow! Big words. Michael should be in the gifted and talented program.

Me and Ryan looked at Michael's map. Michael doesn't like to just walk up and down the street collecting candy like a normal kid. He always plans a careful route so he can go to all the houses that have good candy and not waste any time at the houses where people turn off their lights and pretend they're not home.

Michael is weird.

"We'll save Mrs. Patty's house for last," Michael said. "She says she has more candy than anybody in town. Let's go!"

I was thinking about what Mrs. Patty said earlier at school.

"Do you think there really *is* a Halloween Monster?" I asked the guys as we headed up the street.

"Of course not," Michael said. "Mrs.

Patty was just yanking our chain."

"We'd better be careful just in case," Ryan said.

We set off on our candy quest. There were lots of kids in weird costumes walking up and down the street. Giraffes! Darth Vaders! Two-headed astronauts! Princesses! Cowboys! Ghosts! Four kids dressed up as a bunch of giant bananas! What a freak show!

We saw teenagers dressed up like bums. Teenagers always dress up like bums on Halloween. That must be an easy costume to make, because teenagers dress like bums even when it *isn't* Halloween.

"Trick or treat!" we shouted when we

got to the first house on Michael's map. A lady opened the door.

"Ooh, you boys are scary!" she said, even though she totally didn't look scared at all. "What are you supposed to be?"

"We're a zombie football player, a zombie hockey player, and a killer zombie penguin," Michael said.

"From outer space," I added.

"You can each have a piece of candy," the lady said, holding a bucket out for us.

"Can we take two?" I asked, grabbing a Milky Way.

"Well, okay . . ."

"Can we take four?" I asked, grabbing a Butterfinger.

"No," the lady said, pulling back the bucket.

That lady was mean. We went to the next house and got candy there. Then we went to the house around the corner and got candy there.

Before we went to the next house, each of us took a piece of candy out of our pillowcase and ate it. There's no reason you have to wait until the end of trick-or-treating to start eating your candy. You need to start eating your candy right away, so you'll have enough energy to get *more* candy. That's the first rule of being a kid.

Michael led us a few blocks away to the

next house on his map. He rang the door-bell, and the weirdest thing in the history of the world happened. A lady answered! Well, that wasn't the weird part, because ladies answer doors all the time. The weird part was *who* the lady was.

She wasn't a regular person. She was Mrs. Cooney, our school nurse!

It was weird. I thought Mrs. Cooney lived in the nurse's office. But she lives in a regular house just like a regular person.

"Trick or treat!" we shouted.

"Ooh, I'm scared," Mrs. Cooney said, even though she totally didn't look scared at all.

Mrs. Cooney brought out a bowl filled with apples, carrots, and nuts. Apples, carrots, and nuts? Who gives out apples, carrots, and nuts for Halloween? That's health food!

"You can each take one," Mrs. Cooney said.

"Uh, do we have to?" I asked.

"Don't you have any candy?" asked Michael.

"Candy isn't good for you," said Mrs. Cooney. "It rots your teeth."

"I'd rather have rotten teeth than no candy," I said. But we each took a bag of nuts anyway because that was the closest thing to candy, and we didn't want to hurt Mrs. Cooney's feelings. She doesn't know the first thing about Halloween. You're not supposed to give out healthy food!

Mrs. Cooney is loony.

Luckily, most people gave us candy. But at one house a man gave each of us a quarter instead. He said he ran out of candy. Getting a quarter is almost as good as getting candy because you can use it to *buy* candy.

We had been trick-or-treating for some time when we walked past a spooky

graveyard. That reminded me of the
Halloween Monster again.

Nothing scares me. I would fight a

bear. I would fight a lion. I would fight an elephant. (Well, I don't think elephants fight. If one of them did, I would beat it up.) But I really didn't want to see the Halloween Monster.

It was starting to get a little dark and scary out.

"Hey, if you guys get chopped up by the Halloween Monster," I asked Ryan and Michael, "can I have your candy?"

"There's no such thing as the Halloween Monster, dumbhead," Michael insisted.

But just in case, we made a deal. If one of us was chopped up by the Halloween Monster and the other two survived, they would split the dead kid's candy. And if two of us were chopped up, the kid who lived would get all the candy.

I wondered if Ryan and Michael were secretly hoping that I would get chopped up by the Halloween Monster so they could split my candy. I figured they were probably thinking that, because I was secretly hoping they would get chopped up by the Halloween Monster so I could keep all *their* candy.

It really didn't matter, because each of us was filling our pillowcases with about a million hundred tons of candy. Mine was getting heavy. It would be hard to eat all that candy in one night. But my mom tells me I can accomplish anything if I put my mind to it.

"I'd better eat some more of this candy," I said, reaching into my pillowcase. "It's getting too heavy to carry."

"You'll still be carrying it," Michael said. "It will just be in your stomach."

"But it weighs less in your—"

I never got the chance to finish my sentence because at that very moment, the most terrifying thing in the history of the world happened. A horrible creature jumped out from behind a wall right in front of us.

It was the Halloween Monster!

7

The Halloween Monster!

"Boo!" the horrible creature yelled at us. He was waving his hairy arms around in the air.

"Ahhhhhhhhh!" we screamed. I think the three of us jumped about ten feet high.

"Take our candy!" Ryan yelled. "Take it

all! Just don't kill us."

It was a hideous creature with thick brown hair all over its body. It even had a hairy mask on its face. The only thing the creature was wearing over all that hair was a pair of underwear. Tighty whities.

I thought I was gonna die.

"Are you . . . the Halloween Monster?" I asked, trembling.

"No, dumbhead," the thing said as it took off its mask. "It's *me*."

It was my friend Billy who lives around the corner!

"Hey, that costume is cool!" I told Billy.

"What are you supposed to be?" Ryan asked.

"Take a guess," Billy said.

"A vampire?" guessed Michael.

"Nope."

"A werewolf?" guessed Ryan.

"Nope," said Billy. "I'm the *under*wear-wolf! Get it? A werewolf in his underwear is an underwearwolf!"

Well, the only thing funnier than getting someone to *say* "underwear," or *seeing* someone in their underwear, is a kid *dressed up* as a werewolf in his underwear.

Billy is weird.

"Where are you guys heading?" he asked us. "I'm finished trick-or-treating."

"We're going to 176 Norman Road," Michael said, showing Billy the map. "Our school secretary lives there."

"Oh, you don't want to go *there*," Billy

warned us. "That house is haunted."

"Haunted?" we all asked.

A chill went down my spine. I've been to haunted houses in amusement parks, but I've never been to a *real* haunted house.

"Oh yeah," said Billy. "That lady is a witch. She poisoned her husband, Marvin, and chopped his head off. He came back as a ghost, and he's been driving her insane ever since. She still keeps his head in a bucket down in the basement."

"How do you know all that?" I asked.

"I know everything," Billy claimed. "I'm in the gifted and talented program at my school."

"Wait a minute," Michael said. "Why

did she chop his head off if he was already poisoned?"

"For the fun of it," Billy said. "I told you she's a witch. I'm warning you, stay away from that house."

It was hard for me to imagine Mrs. Patty poisoning her husband or chopping his head off. Every time I get sent to the principal's office, she seems so nice. One time she even gave me a lollipop.

I really wanted to see what kind of candy Mrs. Patty was giving out. But if she chopped my head off, I wouldn't be able to eat the candy anyway. I didn't know what to do.

"I don't believe you," Ryan told Billy. "Mrs. Patty isn't a witch. And she's got more candy than anyone in town. That's what she told us."

"She just told you that so you'll come to her house," Billy said. "Go see for yourself. But don't say I didn't warn you. When she poisons you and chops your heads off, don't come running to me."

Billy left. I put my hand over my neck. Maybe Halloween isn't my favorite holiday after all.

8

The Most Horrible, Dreadful, Disgusting, Repulsive Creature That Ever Walked the Earth

"Maybe we should go home now," I told Michael and Ryan. "We have plenty of candy."

"Go home?" Michael said. "Are you crazy? We haven't been to Mrs. Patty's house yet. She has more candy than anyone in town."

"But what if she chops our heads off?" I asked. "Stuff like that happens all the time, you know."

"She's not going to chop our heads off," Ryan said. "Your friend Billy doesn't know what he's talking about."

"Yeah," Michael said, "and Mrs. Patty told us over and over again that we *have* to trick-or-treat at her house. She might chop off our heads if we *don't* show up."

Good point. Michael really should be in the gifted and talented program.

We kept walking down the street. It was dark now, and scary. I was looking all around, just in case the *real* Halloween Monster jumped out from behind a wall.

"Do you think Mrs. Patty's headless husband, Marvin, still lives with her?" I asked the guys.

"Ghosts have to live *some*where," Michael said. "They're just like regular people, except they're dead."

"I feel sorry for ghosts," said Ryan. "They're like homeless dead people."

We turned the corner onto Norman Road, where Mrs. Patty lives. That's when

I saw the most horrible, dreadful, disgusting, repulsive creature that ever walked the Earth.

It was Andrea Young! She was with her annoying little friend Emily, and they were dressed in their girly costumes. Emily's mom must have sewn that dumb queen outfit together again.

"What are *you* two doing here?" I asked.

"We're trick-or-treating, dumbhead,"

Andrea said. "Just like you."

Andrea and Emily said they were heading for Mrs. Patty's house. I didn't want to walk with them, but it *did* feel safer with five of us walking together.

Finally we got to 176 Norman Road. It was a *big* house. It looked really old, like one of those haunted houses in the movies. There was an iron gate on the outside and some dead trees by the driveway.

"Wow!" Andrea said. "I didn't know school secretaries lived in mansions."

When we got closer, we peeked through the gate and saw

Mrs. Patty's Halloween decorations. There were tombstones sticking out of the lawn. A foot was poking out of a window. There were jack-o'-lanterns with evil faces, spiders hanging from strings, and cats with eyes that lit up. Smoke was coming out of a big pot. Spooky music was coming out of speakers. There was a dummy sitting on a chair on the front porch. (I *hope* it was a dummy, anyway. If that thing moved, I decided, I was going to make a run for it.)

"This place is creepy," said Emily.

Andrea shivered. "Mrs. Patty sure goes all-out when it comes to Hallo—"

But she didn't get to finish her sentence,

because suddenly the front gate squeaked open. Nobody even touched it or anything.

"Come inside. . . ," said a weird man's voice. "If you dare. . . ."

9

Mrs. Patty's Weird House

"Who said that?" Michael asked after we heard the weird man's voice. "Headless Marvin?"

"It wasn't a person," Ryan said. "It was one of those computer voices."

"Let's get out of here," said Emily, "before it's too late!"

She sounded like she was about to cry, as usual. I wanted to cry too, but I didn't want to look like a baby.

"I—I'm not scared," I said.

"M-me neither," said Michael.

We went through the gate and climbed the front steps. You could hardly see anything. Even though I was walking on my tiptoes, the stairs squeaked with every step.

I was trying to find the doorbell when I walked into some spiderwebs. They were all over my face. Yuck! Then I put my foot in something. It was stuck! I couldn't get it out!

"Aaaah!" I screamed, shaking my foot.

"You stepped in a pumpkin head, dork," said Andrea.

"I knew that," I said, finally shaking my foot free.

Any time somebody tells you that you did something dumb, always act like you did it on purpose. That's the first rule of being a kid.

Ryan rang the doorbell. It played funeral music. I was hoping that nobody would be home, but soon we heard footsteps and the front door slowly creaked open. I held my breath.

It was Mrs. Patty. She was still dressed in her witch costume. At least she didn't have an ax.

"Aha," she said in a scary voice, "my last group of trick-or-treaters is finally here."

"I love your Halloween decorations, Mrs. Patty," said Andrea, who never misses a chance to brownnose a grown-up.

"What decorations?" Mrs. Patty said. "My house *always* looks like this."

I was really sweating now.

"We better go," I said. "It's way past our bedtimes."

"Isn't there something you want to say first?" asked Mrs. Patty.

"Yeah," I said, "how does that wart stay on your nose?"

"You're supposed to say 'trick or treat,'" said Mrs. Patty. "Oh," we all said, "trick or treat."

"Before I give you candy," she said, "you must pass a test."

"No, that's not how it goes," said Michael. "All we have to do is say 'trick or treat' and you give us candy. Then we leave. That's the way it's supposed to work."

"Not here," said Mrs. Patty. "Do you want the candy or not?"

"Okay, okay," Ryan said, "what's the test?"

"If you go trick-or-treating," said Mrs. Patty, "and they give out Twix bars at ten houses and Nestlé Crunch bars at five houses and Baby Ruth bars at seven houses, how many candy bars will you have altogether?"

Hey, that was totally not fair! Mrs. Patty was trying to turn trick-or-treating into math class. All day long we have to learn reading and writing and math. My brain is tired after school. I shouldn't have to do more schoolwork. Mrs. Patty isn't even a math teacher. She's a secretary!

"Twenty-two," Andrea answered right away. "You'll have twenty-two candy bars altogether."

"That is correct," Mrs. Patty said as she turned around. "Come in. The candy is down in the basement."

Down in the basement? Why couldn't she just keep a bowl of candy in the front hallway like normal people? Mrs. Patty is batty!

I didn't want to go down in Mrs. Patty's basement. I didn't want to see her husband's head in a bucket down there. It figured that Andrea had to be so good at math. If it weren't for her, we could have left.

Mrs. Patty opened a door and told us to go down the steps. It was dark. I could hardly see anything except some skulls on the walls with candles inside them. When we got to the bottom, we had to walk through a winding hallway. There were doors going off in different directions. I didn't see any candy anywhere. We weren't sure which way to go.

"We're lost!" Andrea said.

"Ouch!" Emily said. "I hit my head on something."

"Let's turn around and make a run for it," I said, "before it's too late."

"I'm scared," Michael said.

"I think I'm going to pee in my pants," said Ryan.

"If I die," Andrea told Emily, "you can have my candy."

"You are a true friend," said Emily. "You can have my candy if I die."

I wished they would both die! I didn't even care if I got their candy or not.

We came to the end of the hallway. There was a door. A sign on the door said, "Candy in Here." I put my hand on the doorknob.

"Don't open that door!" Michael said, just as I was about to turn the doorknob.

"Why not?" I asked.

"In horror movies," Michael explained, "whenever somebody opens a door, a crazy guy wearing a mask leaps out with an ax or something."

"Don't be silly," Ryan said. "Open the door, A.J. We'll get the candy and get out of here."

I looked at Ryan. Emily looked at Andrea. Michael looked at me. I didn't know what to say. I didn't know what to do. I had to think fast. So I turned the doorknob.

Do you want to know what was behind the door?

Well, I'm not going to tell you.

Okay, okay, I'll tell you. But you have to read the next chapter, so nah-nah-nah boo-boo on you.

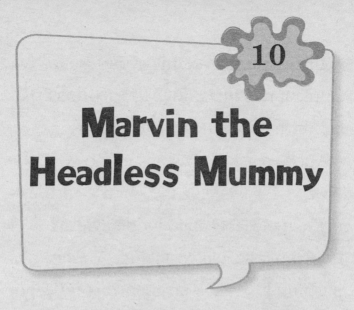

Marvin the Headless Mummy

Behind the door was a big, dark room, and it was full of kids. I couldn't see much, but I recognized Neil the nude kid, and Annette, and some other kids from our class. They were just sitting there, like they were waiting for us.

It was weird.

In the middle of the room was a big trunk. It was like one of those trunks that pirates used to hide their treasure.

Michael asked, "What's in the—

But he never got the chance to finish his sentence, because suddenly the top of the trunk started to lift up. A *hand* was pushing it open! And then this *thing* got out.

It was a mummy . . . with bandages all over its body! But the weird thing was that the mummy didn't have a head! Well, it *had* a head, but the head wasn't on top of its shoulders where it was supposed to be. The mummy was holding its head in its hand like a football!

"Eeeeeeeeeeeeeek!" screamed Emily.

"It's Marvin!" I shouted. "Mrs. Patty's dead husband! His ghost came to life!"

"He's the Halloween Monster!" yelled Ryan.

"We're gonna die!" Michael screamed.

"I *told* you we should have made a run for it!" I shouted.

"Bwa-ha-ha-ha!" said Marvin's head. I had no idea how it was able to talk, but it did. It said, "Give me your candy! Put everything in the trunk, or else."

That head didn't have to ask me twice. I ran over and dumped all the candy from my pillowcase into the trunk. So did Ryan and Michael and Andrea and Emily and Neil the nude kid and Annette. I guess that mummy made *all* the kids turn over their candy, because there were about a million hundred candy bars in the trunk.

"Bwa-ha-ha-ha!" said Marvin's head as Marvin danced around the trunk. "It's mine! All mine! Now at long last I have more candy than anyone in town! My life is complete! Bwa-ha-ha-ha!"

"That's what *you* think!"

We all turned to see who said that. A big guy stepped out of the shadows at the other end of the room. He had a crown on his head and a sword in his hand.

It was Mr. Klutz, our school principal!

"It is I," he said, pointing his sword at Marvin the mummy. "King Louis the

Fourteenth. In the name of France, surrender that candy!"

"Over my dead body!" Marvin said. (That was really weird. Everybody knows mummies are dead bodies to begin with.)

Marvin grabbed a sword off the wall with the hand he wasn't using to hold his own head. Then he and Mr. Klutz started sword fighting, just like in the movies. It was cool.

"Get him, Mr. Klutz!" we all shouted. "Kill the Halloween Monster!"

Mr. Klutz and Marvin were dancing around, swinging their swords at each other.

"Off with your head!" Mr. Klutz said, taking a wild swing.

"His head is already off!" somebody yelled.

"Oh," Mr. Klutz said. "Let him eat cake!"

The sword fight was really exciting. Finally, after a million hundred minutes, Mr. Klutz knocked the sword out of the Halloween Monster's hand.

"Please have mercy," Marvin said as he fell to his knees.

"Begone!" Mr. Klutz said. "Don't ever steal candy from the children of Ella Mentry School again!"

"I'll get you, my pretty," said the Halloween Monster as it ran up the stairs, "and your little dog, too."

"I don't even have a dog," said Mr. Klutz.

After the Halloween Monster ran away, Mrs. Patty came downstairs.

"Hooray for Mr. Klutz!" she yelled. We all started cheering.

"I have defeated the Halloween Monster!" said Mr. Klutz . . . I mean, Louis the Fourteenth.

"We should celebrate!" said Mrs. Patty. "Let's have a candy party!"

"Yeah!" we all yelled.

Mr. Klutz and Mrs. Patty tipped over the treasure chest and dumped all the candy on the floor. We were allowed to eat whatever we wanted and take the rest home.

I ate so much candy, I thought I was
going to throw up. It was the greatest
night of my life.

After eating all that candy, I couldn't fall asleep for a million hundred hours. I just lay there in bed thinking about all the cool stuff that happened.

Maybe Mrs. Patty does keep her Halloween decorations up all year round. Maybe her husband, Marvin, really is dead. Maybe she did chop his head off and turn him into a mummy. Maybe that's why he's so mad and he has to run around the house holding his own head. Maybe now that he lost the sword fight to Mr. Klutz, he'll be nicer and stop taking kids' candy. Maybe Marvin and Mrs. Patty will get back together and just be normal people again, even though one of them is dead. And maybe Mrs. Patty will be able to get that wart off her nose.

But it won't be easy!

Check out the **My Weird School** series!

#1: Miss Daisy Is Crazy!
Pb 0-06-050700-4

The first book in the hilarious series stars A.J., a second grader who hates school—and can't believe his teacher hates it too!

#2: Mr. Klutz Is Nuts!
Pb 0-06-050702-0

A.J. can't believe his crazy principal wants to climb to the top of the flagpole!

#3: Mrs. Roopy Is Loopy!
Pb 0-06-050704-7

The new librarian at A.J.'s weird school thinks she's George Washington one day and Little Bo Peep the next!

#4: Ms. Hannah Is Bananas!
Pb 0-06-050706-3

Ms. Hannah, the art teacher, wears clothes made from pot holders and collects trash. Worse than that, she's trying to make A.J. be partners with yucky Andrea!

#5: Miss Small Is off the Wall!
Pb 0-06-074518-5

Miss Small, the gym teacher, is teaching A.J.'s class to juggle scarves, balance feathers, and do everything but play sports!

#6: Mr. Hynde Is Out of His Mind!
Pb 0-06-074520-7

The music teacher, Mr. Hynde, raps, break-dances, and plays bongo drums on the principal's bald head! But does he have what it takes to be a real rock-and-roll star?

#7: Mrs. Cooney Is Loony!
Pb 0-06-074522-3

Mrs. Cooney, the school nurse, is everybody's favorite—but is she hiding a secret identity?

#8: Ms. LaGrange Is Strange!
Pb 0-06-082223-6

The new lunch lady, Ms. LaGrange, talks funny—and why is she writing secret messages in the mashed potatoes?

#9: Miss Lazar Is Bizarre!
Pb 0-06-082225-2

What kind of grown-up likes cleaning throw-up? Miss Lazar is the weirdest custodian in the history of the world!

#10: Mr. Docker Is off His Rocker!
Pb 0-06-082227-9

Mr. Docker, the science teacher, alarms and amuses A.J.'s class with his wacky experiments and nutty inventions.

#11: Mrs. Kormel Is Not Normal!
Pb 0-06-082229-5

A.J.'s school bus gets a flat tire, then becomes hopelessly lost at the hands of Mrs. Kormel, the wacky bus driver.

#12: Ms. Todd Is Odd!
Pb 0-06-082231-7

Something weird is going on! Has the substitute teacher kidnapped Miss Daisy?

Also look for...
#14: Miss Holly Is Too Jolly!

📖 HarperTrophy®
An Imprint of HarperCollins*Publishers*

www.dangutman.com